HELLO KITTY'S BEDTIME SEARCH

by Sarah Bright • illustrated by Scott Sullivan

RANDOM HOUSE 🏠 NEW YORK

Copyright © 1982 by Sanrio Co. Ltd. All rights reserved under International and Pan-American Copyright Conventions. Published in the United States by Random House, Inc., New York, and simultaneously in Canada by Random House of Canada Limited, Toronto. *Library of Congress Cataloging in Publication Data:* Bright, Sarah. Hello Kitty's bedtime search. SUMMARY: As she searches for her bear just before bedtime, Kitty locates some forgotten favorite things. [1. Lost and found possessions—Fiction. 2. Bedtime—Fiction] I. Sullivan, Scott, 1952– ,ill. II. Title. PZ7.B7652He [E] 82-3719 AACR2 ISBN: 0-394-85397-0 Manufactured in the United States of America 1 2 3 4 5 6 7 8 9 0

Every night, when Kitty went to bed, she took Lucy, her best bear. But one night Kitty couldn't find Lucy.

Kitty looked under the bed.
Lucy wasn't there.

Under the bed Kitty found her striped woolen knee socks. She put them on.

Then Kitty looked in her
toy box. Lucy wasn't there.

In the toy box Kitty found her old necklace. It wouldn't fit over her head anymore, so she wound it around her arm.

Then Kitty looked in her
drawer. Lucy wasn't there.

But Kitty found her purple T-shirt. She had forgotten she had it, so she put it on.

Kitty was happy to find so many old things she had forgotten about. But she still wanted Lucy. Kitty felt very sad.

"I can't go to sleep without her," said Kitty.

"Don't worry, Kitty. Lucy will turn up," said Mama. She helped Kitty take off the purple T-shirt, the old necklace, and the striped socks.

Mama helped Kitty into bed and tucked her under the quilt. Kitty felt a lump, a lump that was soft and furry.

Lucy!

Kitty was so happy to find her. Kitty held Lucy and fell fast asleep.